NATIVE NORTHWEST

ART BY INDIGENOUS ARTISTS

NativeNorthwest.com • Vancouver, Canada • 604-266-9044 • info@nativenorthwest.com
Printed in Canada using soy-based inks and non-toxic coatings.
Paper sourced from sustainable forests.
ISBN 978-1-55476-288-0 • Third printing, January 2020
Book Design by Kylie Ward
Partial proceeds from this publication support Aboriginal learning programs.

Goodnight World

Animals of the Native Northwest

"Goodnight world
rest in peace
wake up renewed
embrace the magic that we live in
blessings to all that surrounds us
respect all that is offered
share the spirit within"

–Corey Bulpitt, Haida

"For thousands of years we have shared the rainforest with an abundance of wildlife. We have observed these animals and have learned to live with them in balance and harmony. Animals are critical to our culture and to our people. Our ancestors passed down many stories and traditions about our intimate connection to animals. In honouring our ancestors' traditions, I create art that passes down our world view to our children and grandchildren and shares our culture with a wider audience."

–Doug LaFortune, Coast Salish

Contents

The following 26 First Nations and Native artists have been generous in sharing their art and culture. In order of appearance, top to bottom, left to right:

Goodnight sun
lowering in the sky.

Goodnight butterflies
stretching your wings before bed.

Goodnight birds
singing each other to sleep.

Goodnight frogs
croaking into the night.

Goodnight bugs
resting after a busy day.

Goodnight sea creatures
rocking gently with the waves.

Goodnight turtles
moving quietly in your shells.

Goodnight fish
floating while you rest.

Goodnight whales
humming softly in the sea.

Goodnight bears
finding shelter in the forest.

Goodnight beavers
dreaming together
in your lodge.

Goodnight owls
keeping watch through the night.

Goodnight wolves
howling in harmony
to the moon.

Goodnight animals of
the sky, land and sea.